DC™ SUPER-PETS!

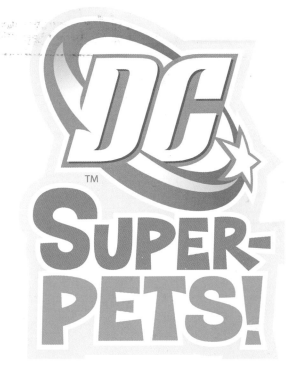

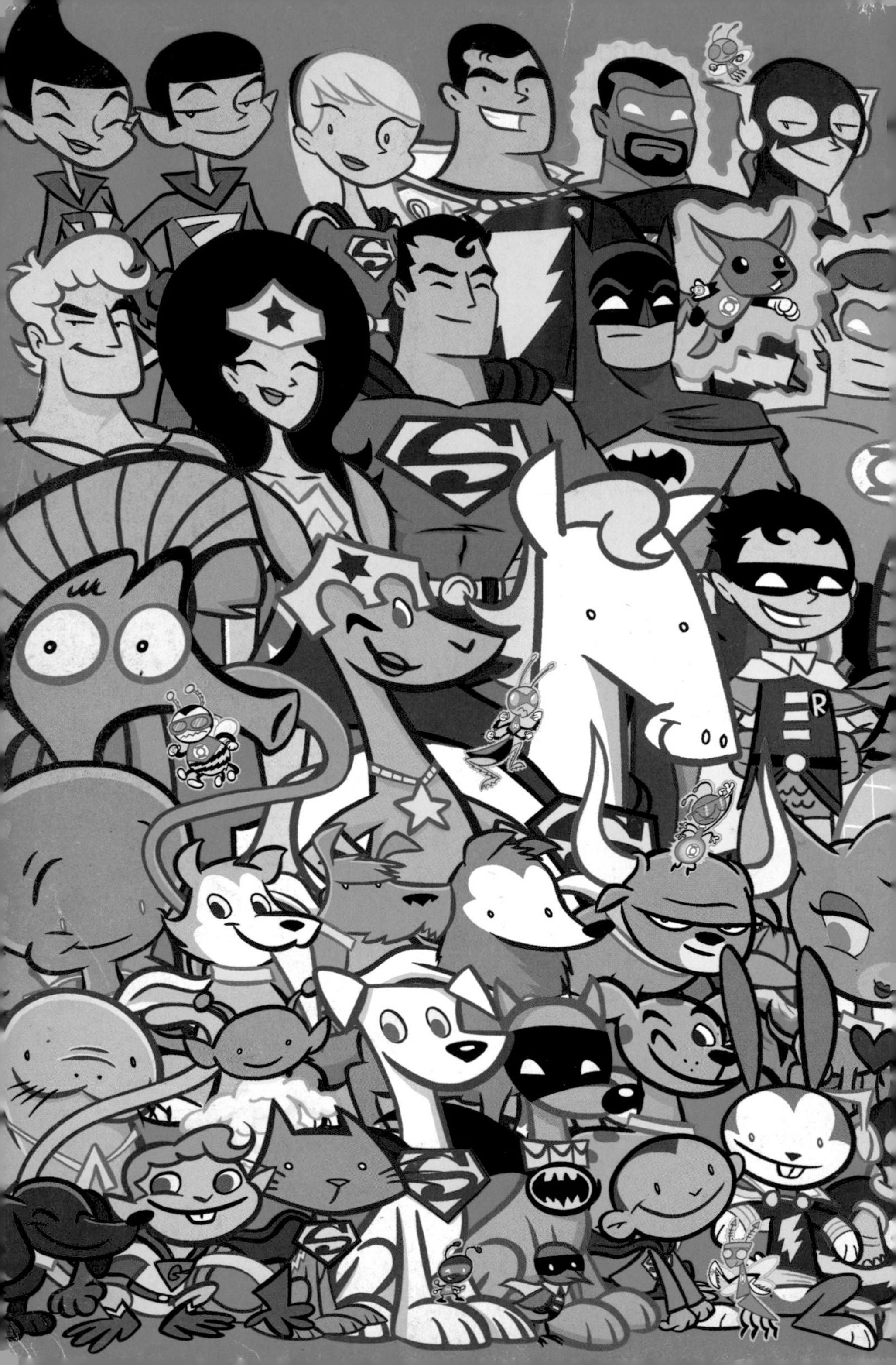

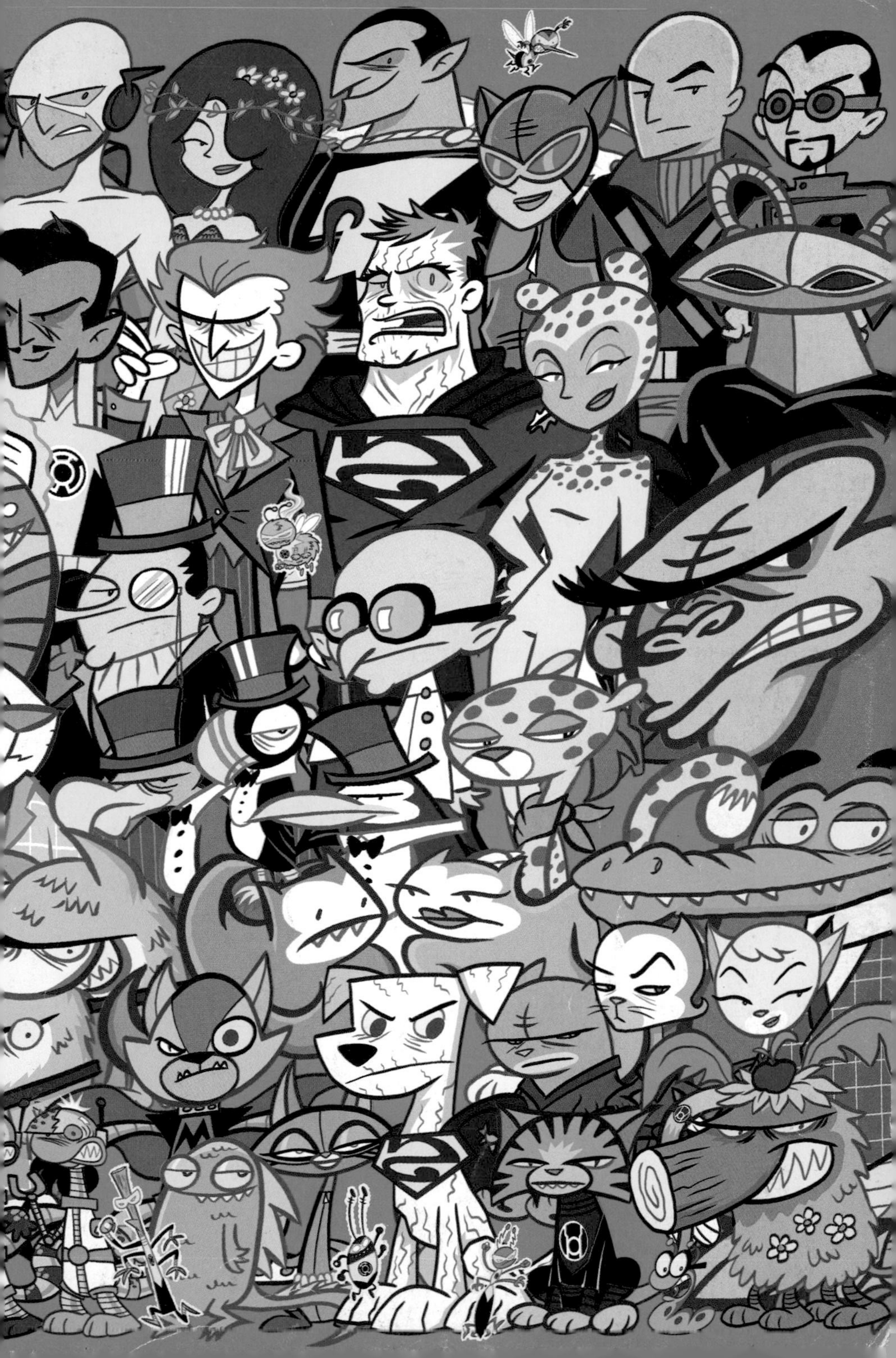

DC™

SUPER-PETS!

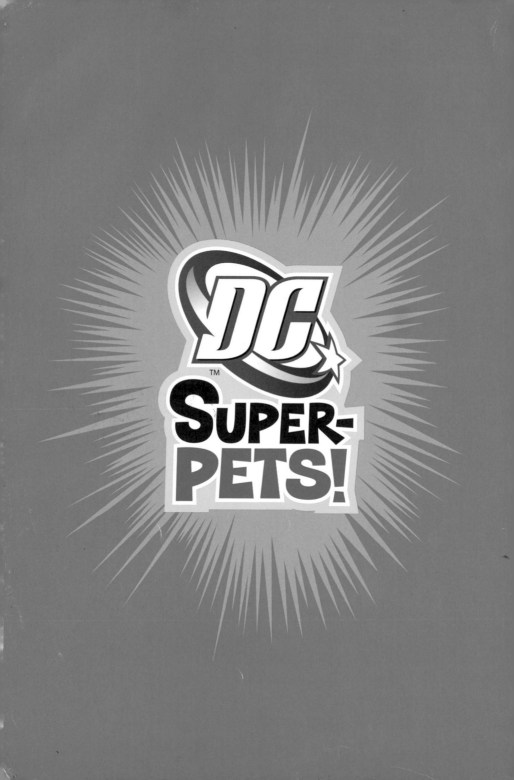

by Sarah Hines Stephens

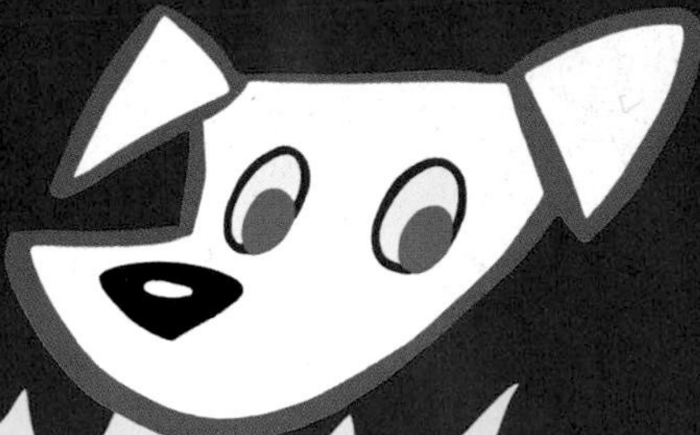

BACKWARD BOWWOW

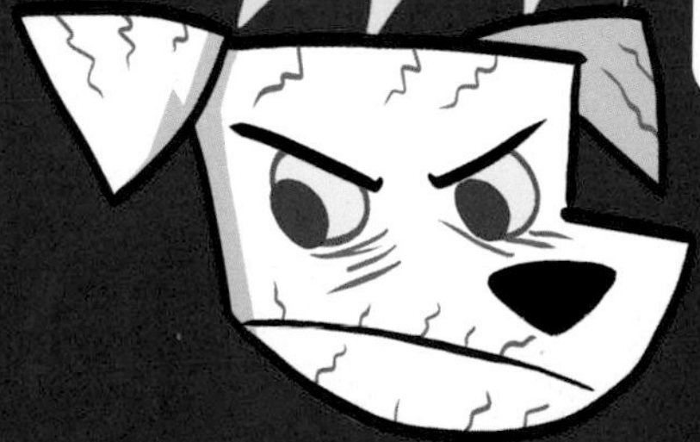

illustrated by Art Baltazar

Superman created by Jerry Siegel and Joe Shuster

Picture Window Books™
a capstone imprint

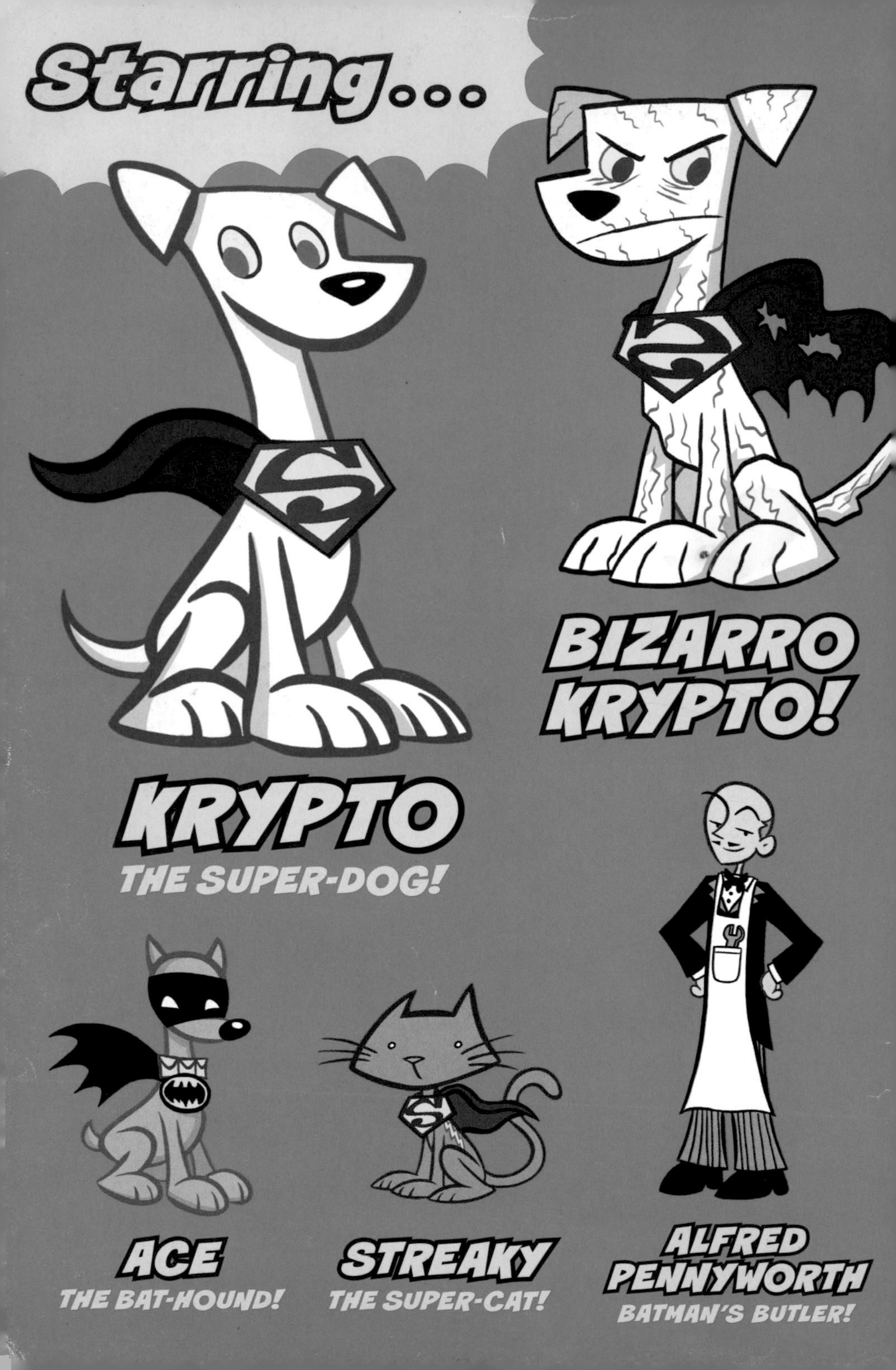
Starring...
KRYPTO
THE SUPER-DOG!
BIZARRO KRYPTO!
ACE
THE BAT-HOUND!
STREAKY
THE SUPER-CAT!
ALFRED PENNYWORTH
BATMAN'S BUTLER!

TABLE OF CONTENTS!

Meet Krypto! **4**

Chapter 1
BACKWARD PLANET   6

Chapter 2
A SHOCKING DISPLAY   19

Chapter 3
NONSENSE   37

More fun! **50-56**

SUPER-PET HERO FILE 001: KRYPTO

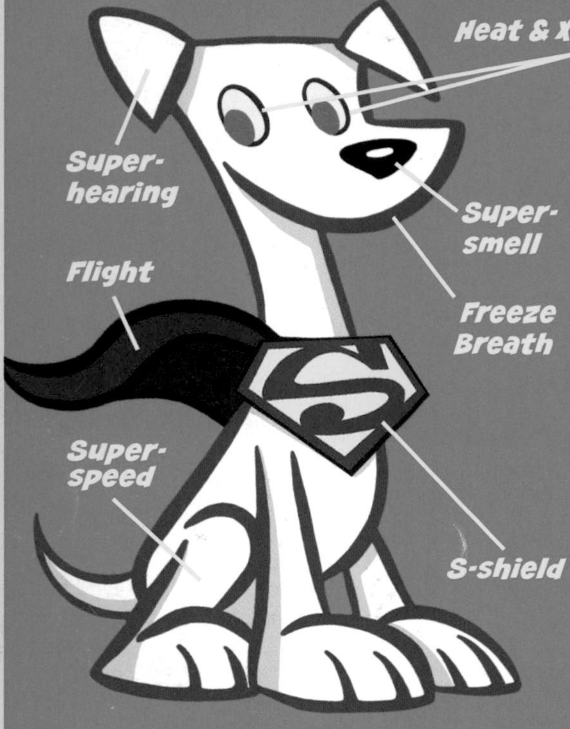
Heat & X-ray Vision
Super-hearing
Super-smell
Flight
Freeze Breath
Super-speed
S-shield

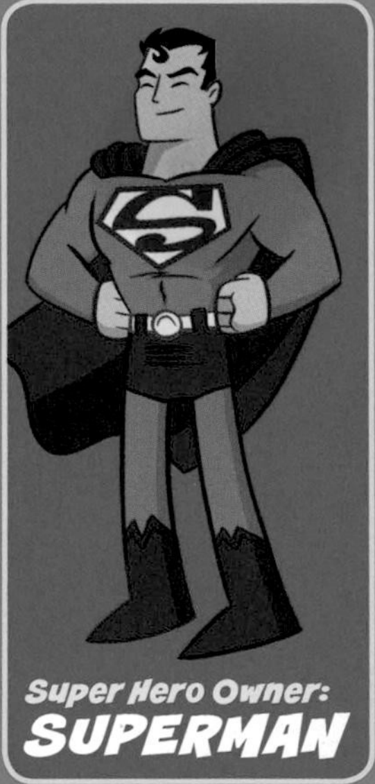
Super Hero Owner:
SUPERMAN

Species: Super-Dog
Place of Birth: Krypton
Weakness: Kryptonite
Favorite Food: Ka-pow Chow!

Bio: The childhood pet of the Man of Steel, Krypto the Super-Dog has the same powers as his heroic master.

SUPER-PET ENEMY FILE 001:
BIZARRO KRYPTO

Ice & X-ray Vision

Super-hearing

Flight

Super-smell

Flame Breath

Super-speed

Backward S-shield

Super-villain Owner:
BIZARRO

Bio: When Krypto the Super-Dog crashed on Htrae, the Bizarros created his evil twin called Bizarro Krypto.

Species: Bizarro Dog

Place of Birth: Htrae

Weakness: Blue Kryptonite

Favorite Food: Pineapple Upside-down Cake

Chapter 1

BACKWARD PLANET

SMAAAASH!

Shortly after midnight, an alien shuttle crashed down in the city of Metropolis. The strange rocket ship scraped across a mall parking lot. A trail of sparks streamed out behind it.

SKREEECH! The shuttle skidded to a halt next to a dumpster. A door in the side of the craft opened, and out stepped a white dog. The alien canine had a large head and red eyes. He was strong and wore a flowing red cape.

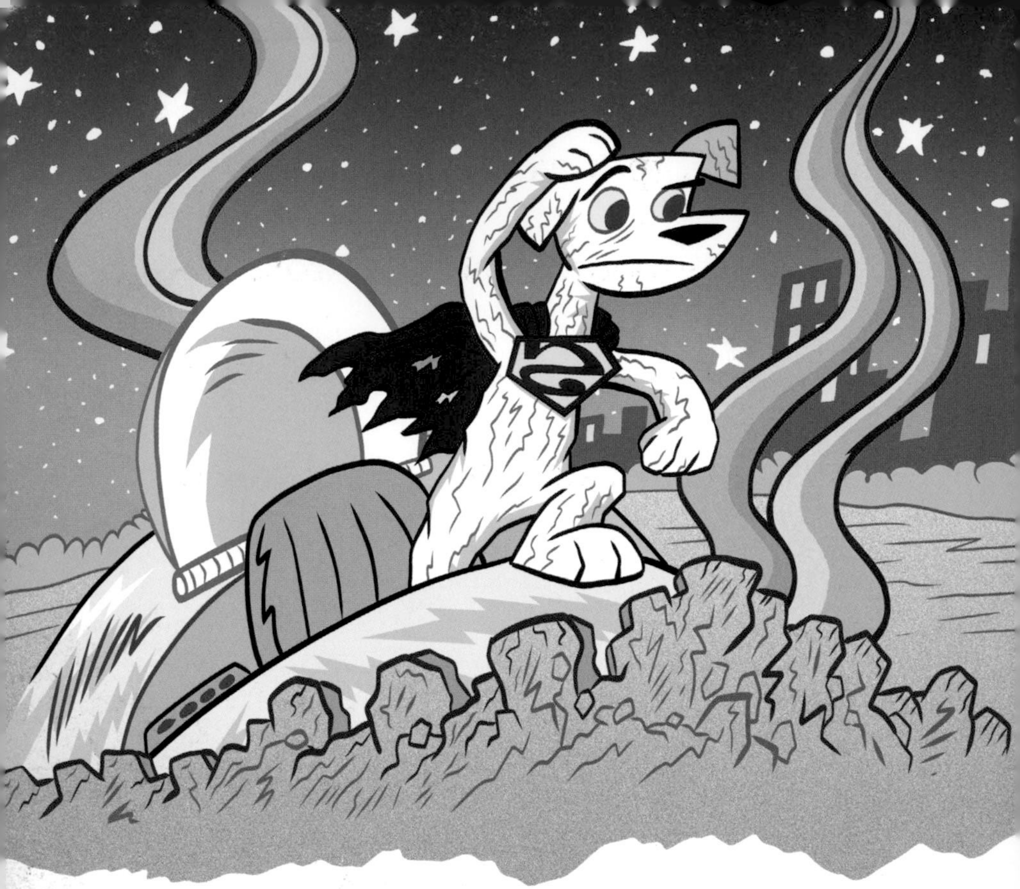

The alien looked a lot like Krypto the Super-Dog. But he was not Krypto. He was actually the exact opposite.

He was **Bizarro Krypto!** And he had never meant to land on Earth.

Bizarro Krypto was the only passenger onboard a shuttle from the planet **Htrae**. The shuttle had flown far off course. It had gotten caught in the Earth's gravity.

From the space ship's window, Bizarro Krypto had watched the round planet growing closer and closer. It looked very, very different from his home planet.

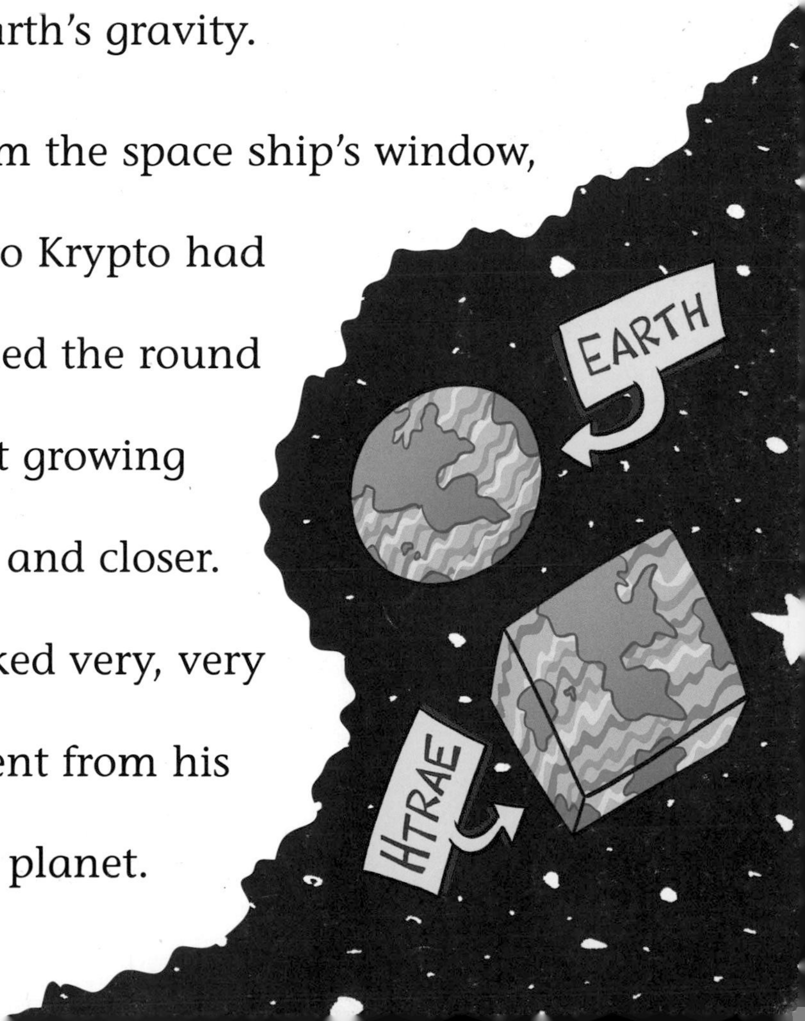
EARTH
HTRAE

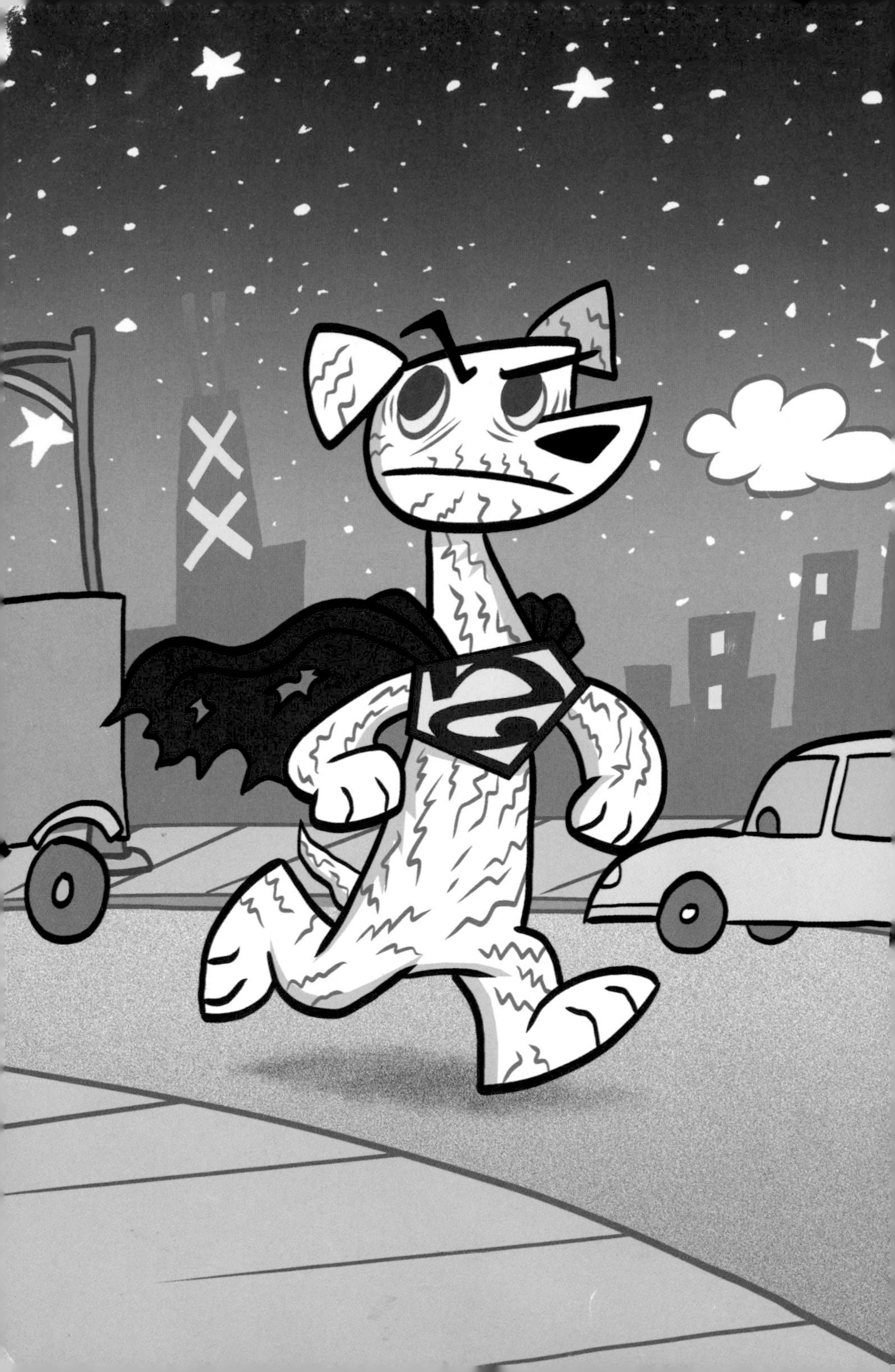

"Good bumpy landing," said Bizarro Krypto. The alien canine climbed out of the shuttle.

FWIP! FWIP! FWIP! FWIP!

He shook himself off. Then he walked into the middle of the mall parking lot.

The moon was full. The parking lot was empty and the stores were closed. Bizarro Krypto started to worry. On Htrae, the stores were always busy at night. Where was everyone?

Bizarro Krypto followed the sidewalk through Metropolis. He passed more closed stores. He passed more dark houses full of sleeping people.

Bizarro Krypto did not understand why people would sleep at night!

Moments later, the sun started to rise. People began to wake up. Bizarro Krypto was stunned by what he saw in the light. Peeking in windows, he saw dogs lying and eating on the floor. Humans read on couches and sat at tables.

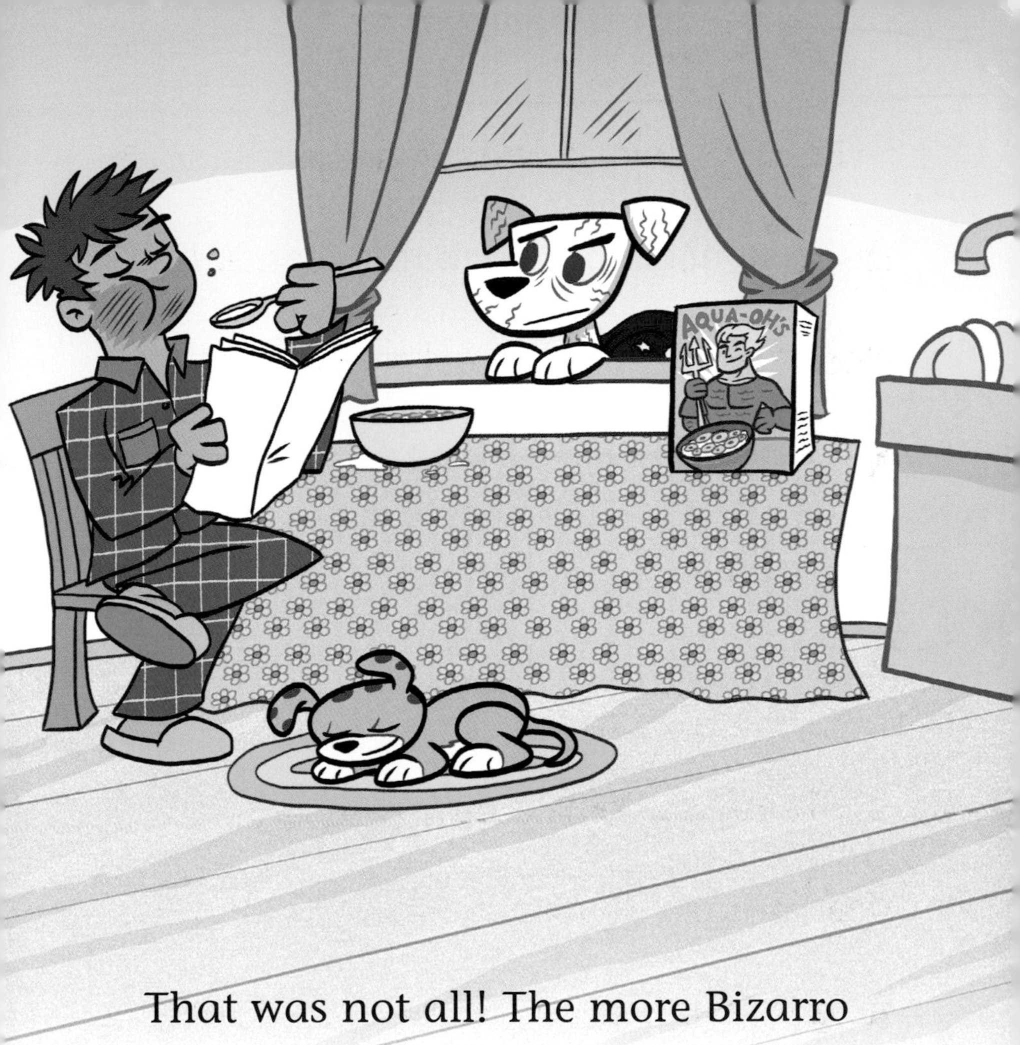
AQUA-OH'S

That was not all! The more Bizarro Krypto looked, the more confused and worried he became. The people and animals on this round planet were all backward. **Nothing made any sense!**

Bizarro Krypto was about to head back to his ship. Suddenly, a man in a bathrobe opened his door nearby. A small puppy scampered out.

Bizarro Krypto stopped to watch what would happen next. The young dog picked up a newspaper and trotted back to drop it at the man's feet.

"RUFF! RUFF! RUFF!"

"Good dog!" said the man.

Then the owner reached down and patted his dog. He handed the pet a chew bone.

Bizarro Krypto thought it was weird for a dog to bring a newspaper to a person. On Htrae, people gave papers to dogs so they could chew them and make reading the news harder.

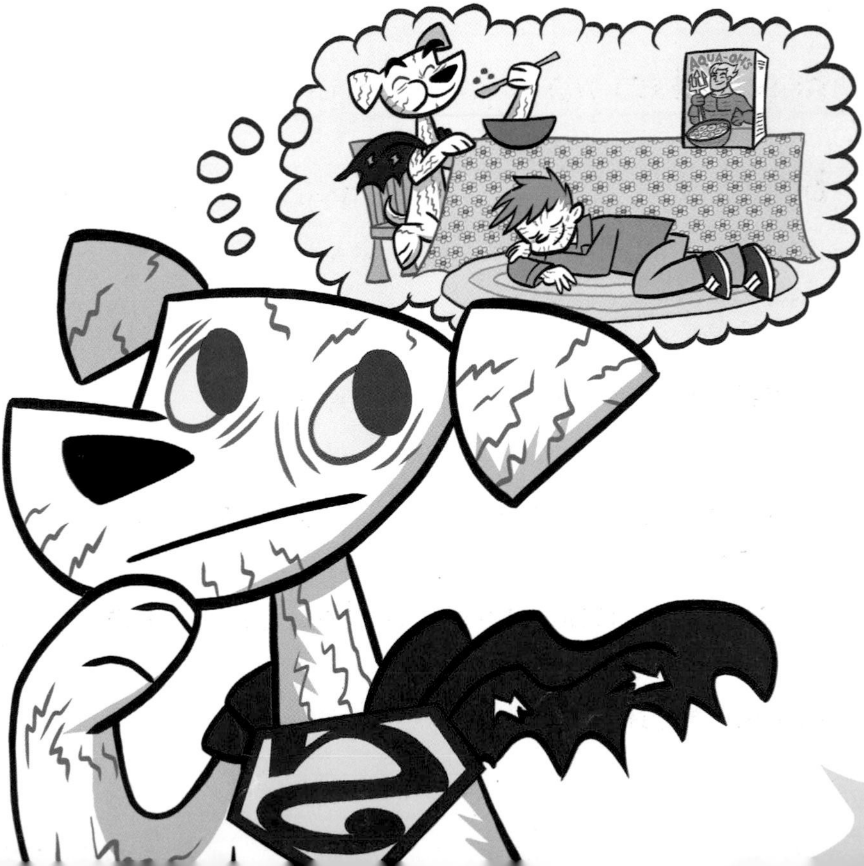
AQUA-OH'S

Still, that was not the strangest thing Bizarro Krypto saw! As he watched, the small dog took the bone. She ran off and dug a hole in the yard. **PLOP!** Then she dropped the bone in it!

Bizarro Krypto couldn't take it. 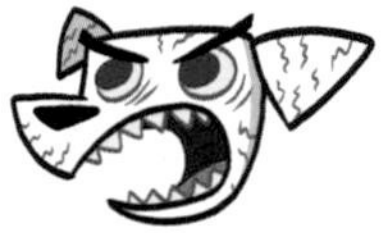 **"Stop,"** he barked. **"You no do that!"**

The chew bone belonged in a frame. It was nasty and ugly and needed to be on display so all could enjoy it!

The little dog looked up, confused. "I'm saving it for later," she said shyly.

"No, no, no!" Bizarro Krypto said.

He didn't have time to explain what
the dog was doing wrong. She ran off
barking toward the fence.

Bizarro Krypto could not believe his
eyes. The dog was chasing after a cat!

Bizarro Krypto was more baffled than ever. What was a dog doing chasing a cat? It was like nothing he had ever seen.

Feeling a little shaken up, Bizarro Krypto walked toward downtown. **The creatures of Earth needed his help.**

Chapter 2

A SHOCKING DISPLAY

The people and animals of Earth were starting their day. Bizarro Krypto thought they were doing it all wrong.

He had never seen dogs wearing collars. Collars were for humans! He had never seen people walk dogs on leashes. Those were for humans, too!

Then Bizarro Krypto saw the most shocking thing of all. Through the windows at the Museum of Natural History, the alien dog spotted an enormous skeleton. It was a dinosaur skeleton, clean and shiny.

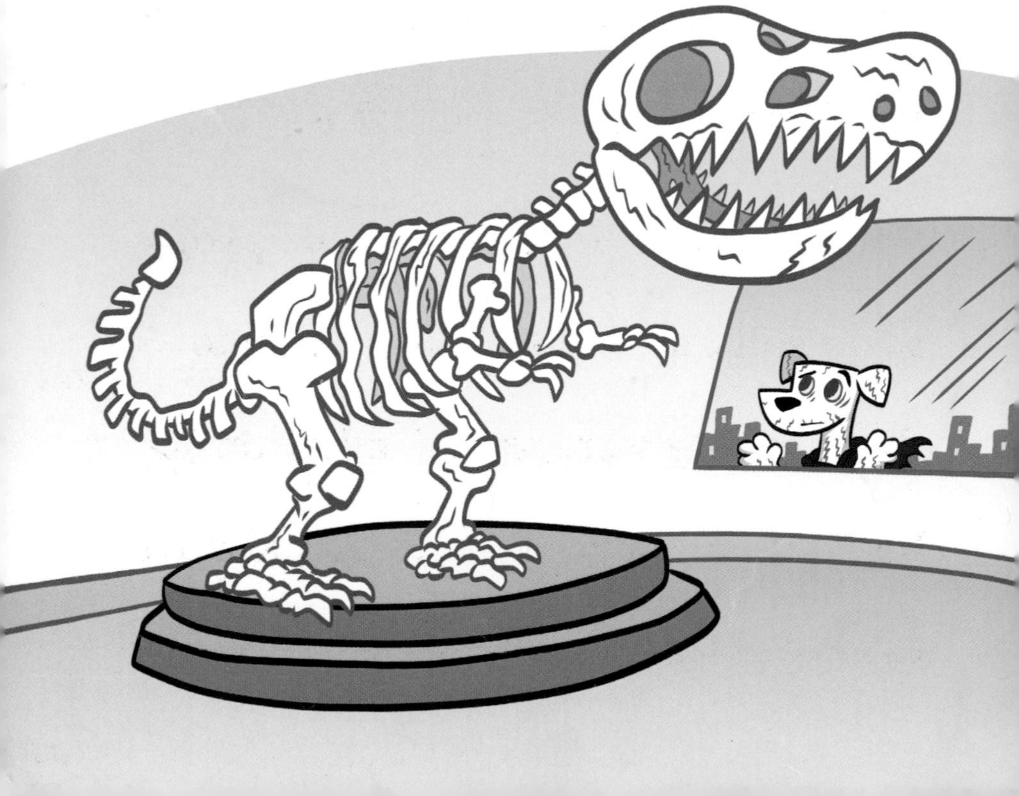

"That not good," Bizarro Krypto growled. **"That not good at all."**

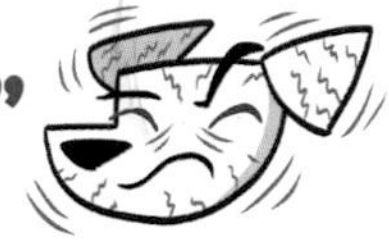

On Htrae, big dry bones like those had to be buried. Only meaty, stinky bones were hung up for display. Huge bones like those in the museum, without anything to chew on, were too terrifying to show to the public.

Below the enormous skeleton, people stood still and stared. Bizarro Krypto thought they were frozen in horror. He had to help them. Nobody should have to look at such awful bones!

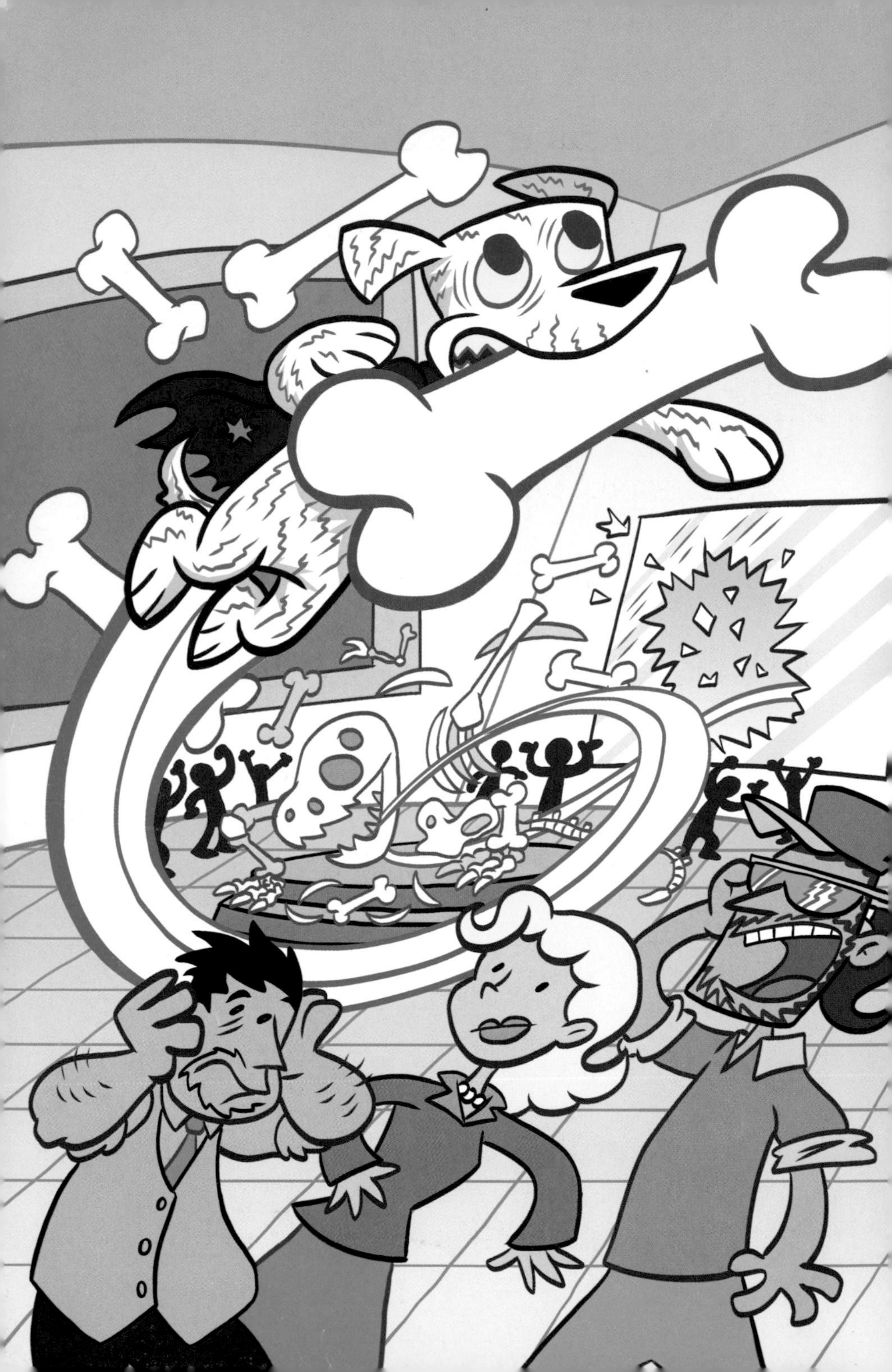

With incredible speed, Bizarro

Krypto burst into the museum.

He grasped one of the giant bones

in his jaws and flew toward the exit.

Alarms sounded. People screamed.

"They happy," he said. "I helping."

Outside, Bizarro Krypto spotted a

large grassy area. It was the city park.

THUD! He touched down and started

digging. Dirt flew out of the hole faster

than wind from a hurricane. **FWOOOM!**

When the hole was finished, Bizarro Krypto flew back and forth carrying bones. He'd dug a pit so huge a house could have fit inside! Soon, he would have all of the big bones hidden in it. The Earth people would be safe.

Bizarro Krypto was proud. He did not hear the sirens coming.

WEE-OOO! WEE-OOO!

"Stop! Police!" one of the officers shouted. Six police had formed a line to block Bizarro Krypto from going back into the museum.

Bizarro Krypto didn't stop. He flew right past the police. **WHOOSH!** They tried to catch him in a net, but it was useless against the dog's alien powers.

"We need help!" one of the police officers shouted.

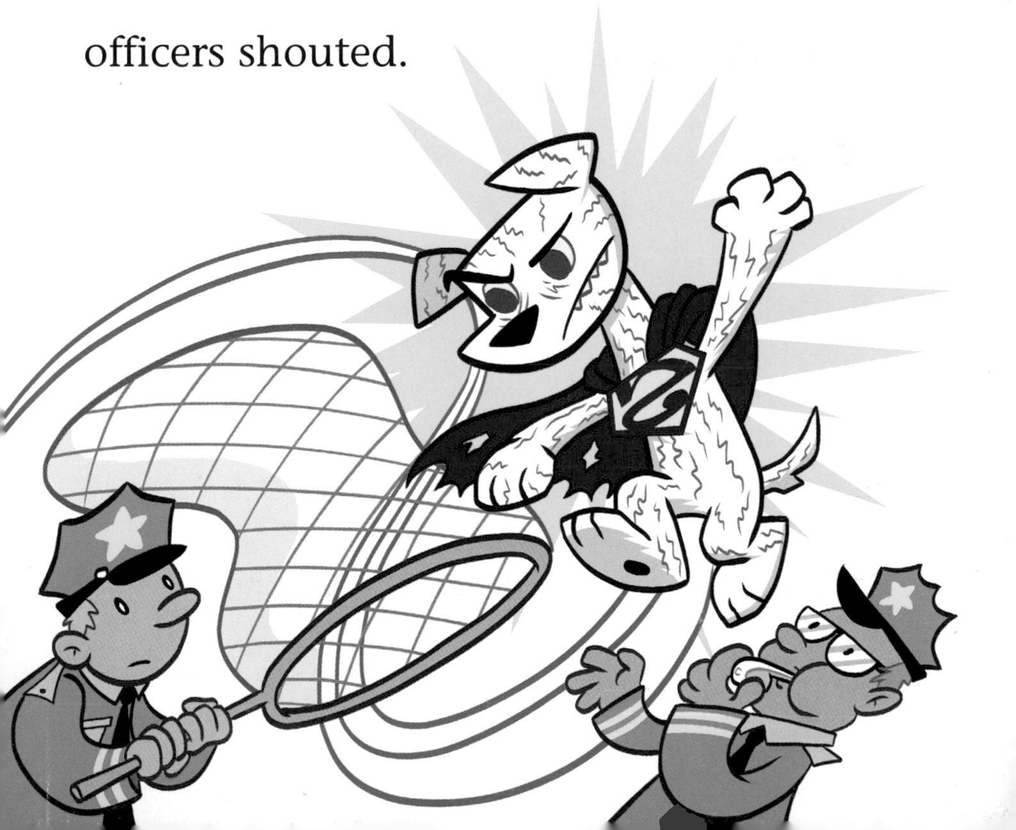

The officer was right. The only Earth creatures with enough power to stop a Bizarro dog were a pack of Super-Pets.

One of the officers put out the call, and just in time. Inside the museum, Bizarro Krypto had begun to pull apart the skeleton of a whale.

Moments later, the real **Krypto the Super-Dog** and **Ace the Bat-Hound** arrived at the scene.

"Let's go!" Krypto barked. "That crazy dog is destroying the museum!"

“Wait,” Ace cautioned. “He looks a little like you.”

Krypto shook it off. “No he doesn’t,” he said gruffly. **“He’s a bad guy. Bad guys don’t look like me.”**

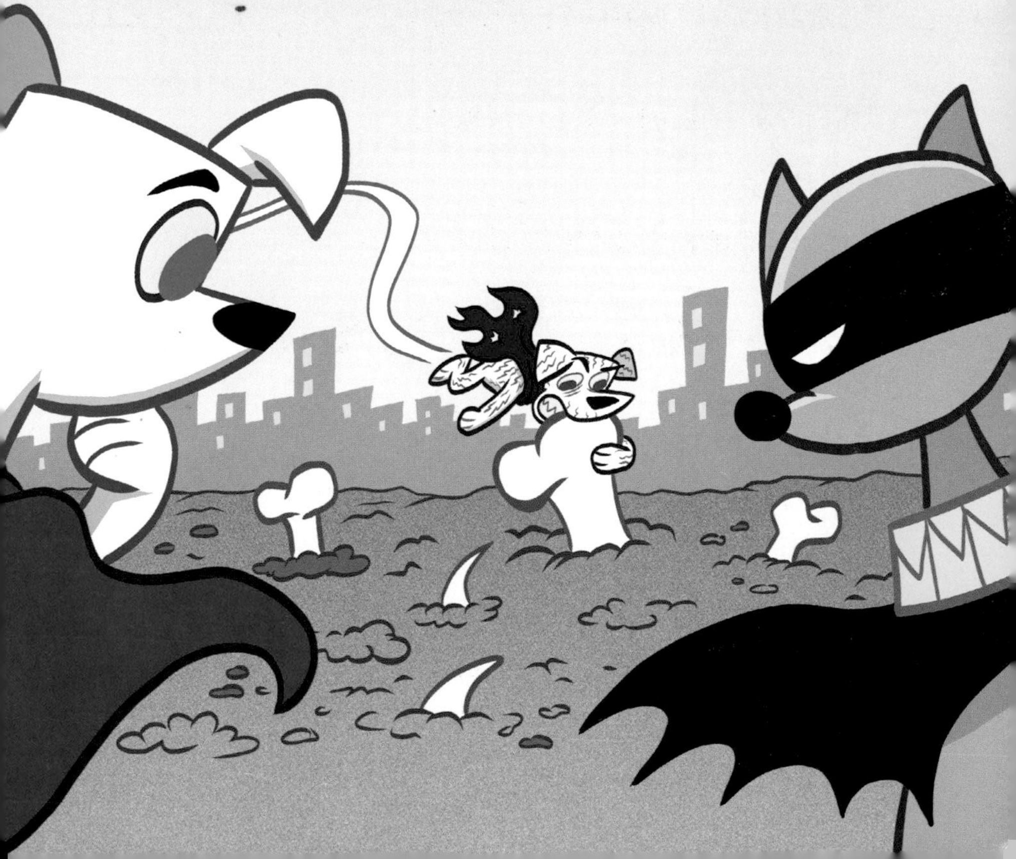

Ace did not move. He was a good detective. He wanted to wait a moment to figure out what was happening.

Through his mask, Ace watched Bizarro Krypto flying back and forth, hauling and burying bones. He definitely did look like Krypto. But he didn't act like him.

The people at the museum had started throwing trash at the strange dog, trying to make him stop. Their attention only made him tear down the displays faster.

"You no have to say thank you," 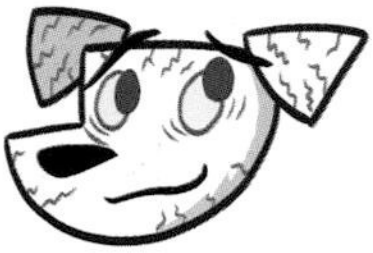 Bizarro Krypto told the crowd. He ducked his head shyly. But the people didn't understand him.

Bizarro Krypto thought they were being nice. On Htrae, throwing trash was a way to show how much you liked something.

Ace didn't know this. **All he knew was that something was very wrong.** 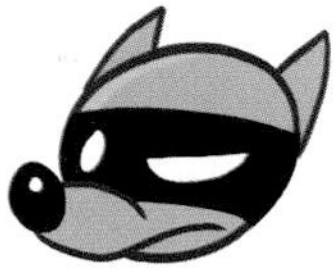

"Come on! Let's stop this pooch already," Krypto said. 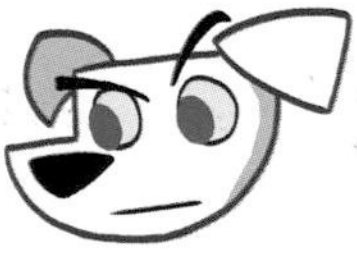

"We can give it a shot," Ace agreed. "But there's more going on here than meets the eye."

Krypto had no idea what his friend was talking about. The Super-Dog stepped out to block the Bizarro's path. Krypto unleashed a blast of icy breath to stop this backward dog in his tracks.

SWOOOOSH!

Bizarro Krypto dropped his bone. Then he fired a warm blast of his own. The two streams of air met, creating a swirling vortex. **It was a standoff!**

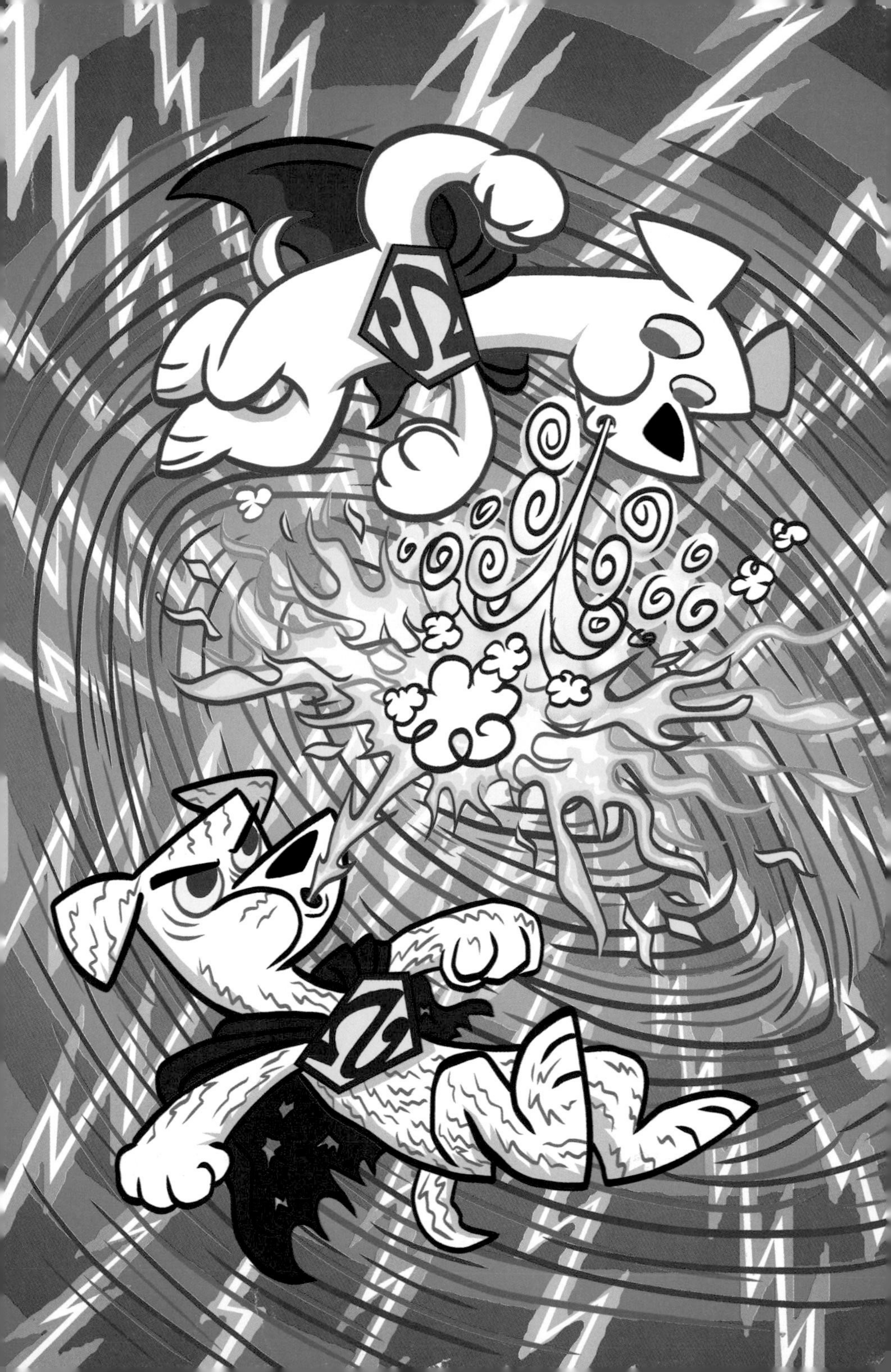

While Krypto and his reverse twin were busy, Ace moved. He snagged the stolen bone and dragged it back toward the museum. The crowd that had gathered gave him a loud cheer.

Bizarro Krypto caught on. He sent one last blast of hot breath at Krypto and turned to face the Bat-Hound.

"Bad dog," Bizarro Krypto barked at the Super-Pet. **"You frighten poor people. Bad."**

The backward bowwow grabbed the bone back, snatching it easily. Then he flew toward the giant hole he'd dug.

"I helping," said Bizarro Krypto.

"Helping?" Ace repeated the word to himself. **"Bad dog."**

Then Ace remembered something.
Batman had told him about **Bizarro**
World once. His crime-fighting partner
had explained that the **Bizarros** were
different from earthlings. Their world
was the exact opposite of Earth.

The trouble was, their ways made no
sense here. Batman had also explained
to Ace that because the Bizarros were
just as strong and powerful as Earth's
super heroes, they were extremely
hard to control. Their ideas could be
harmful even if they meant well.

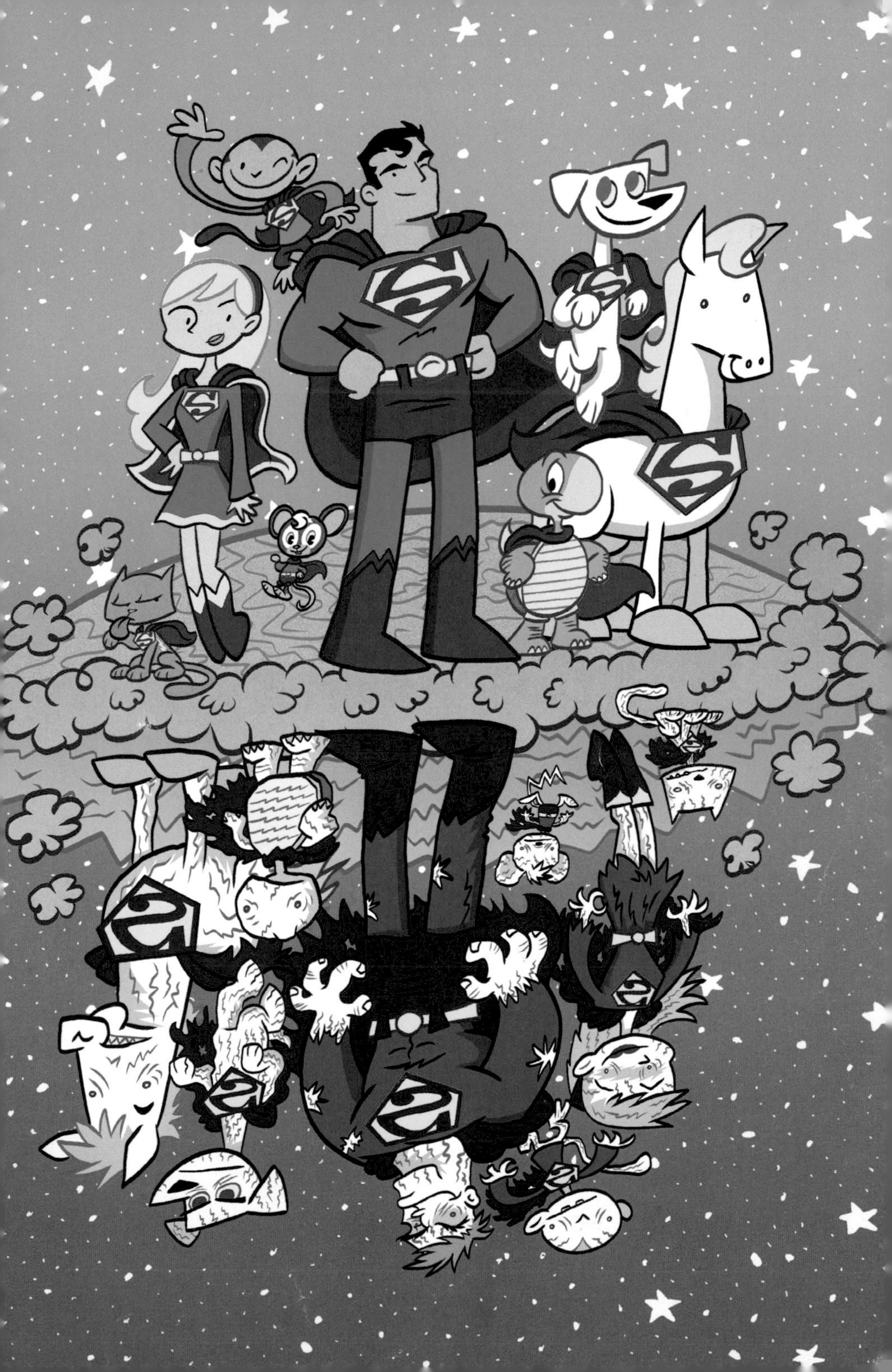

If this other Krypto was a Bizarro from Htrae, the best thing the Super-Pets could do would be to send him home. **But how?**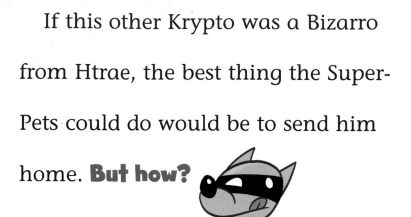

Chapter 3

NONSENSE

"**Krypto!**" Ace called to his friend. "Keep an eye on Bizarro. I'll be back."

Without stopping to explain, Ace took off. He had to find whatever had brought Bizarro Krypto to Earth. They were going to need it to send the backward bowwow home again.

Krypto watched Ace running down the street. He was not sure what the other dog was doing, but he knew Ace liked to have a plan. He also knew that Ace's plans were usually good.

All Krypto needed to worry about was his odd opposite. Drawing a deep breath, he turned and tried again to freeze Bizarro Krypto in his tracks. Bizarro Krypto fought back with fiery breath. **FWOOOOOM!**

Oh well, Krypto thought. ***If I can't stop him, at least I can keep him busy.***

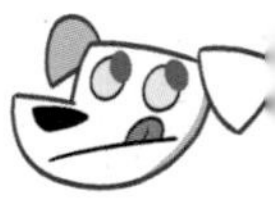

Krypto was drawing a big breath when he picked up a new sound with his sensitive ears. It was the soothing purr of a cat.

"Streaky!" shouted the Super-Dog.

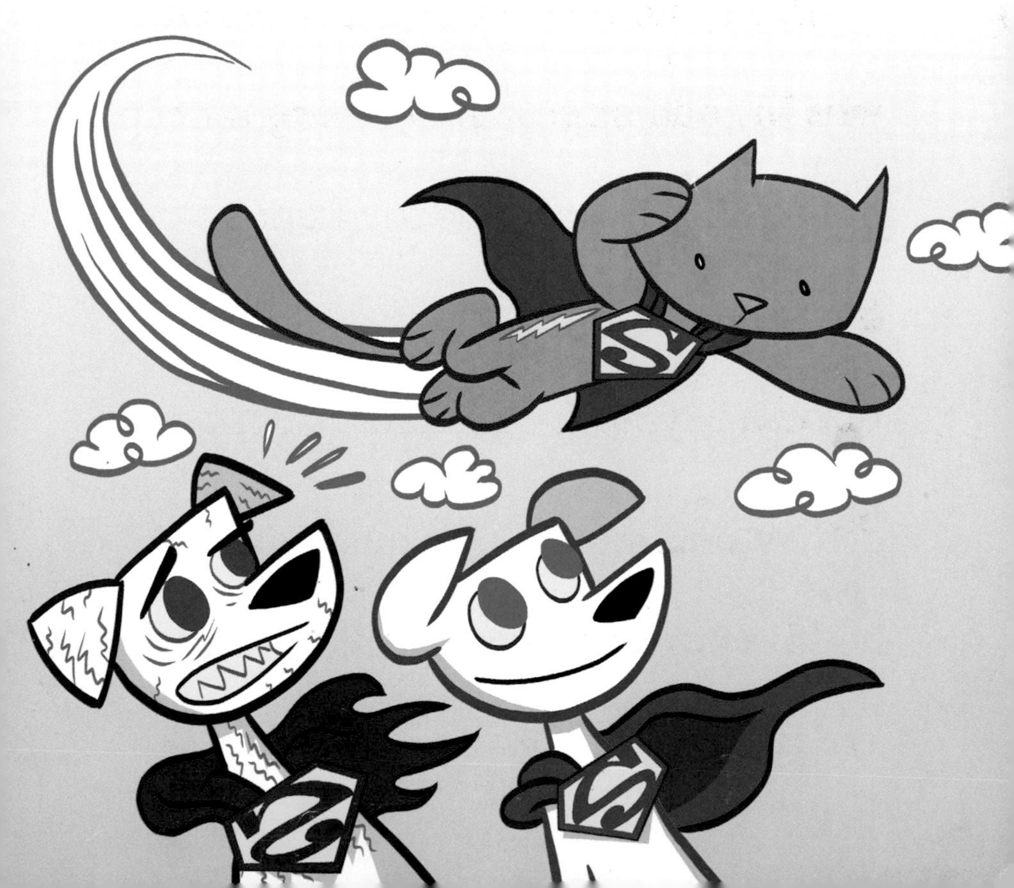

Krypto was relieved that another Super-Pet was coming to join him, but he was not sure Streaky would be much help.

Supergirl's orange cat did not leave his home often. He liked to nap during the day and fight crime at night. Still, it was a good thing he had answered the call.

The Super-Dog was just about to deliver one more chilly gust when he saw Bizarro Krypto **freeze in his tracks.**

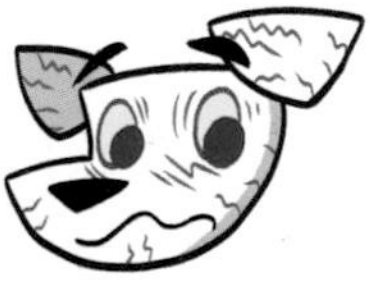

WHUMP!

Streaky landed beside the Super-Dog. **"What's the problem?"** he asked, casually licking his paw.

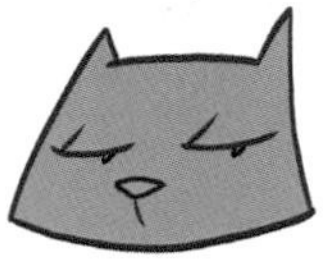

Krypto didn't answer. He was staring at Bizarro Krypto.

The alien dog still had not moved. His eyes were wide. He tried to blow out another hot breath, but coughed and staggered backward instead.

He was afraid of something, and that something had to be Streaky!

Krypto had seen dogs that were afraid of Streaky before, but usually not until the cat revealed his powers. Bizarro Krypto was freaked out before Streaky had done a thing.

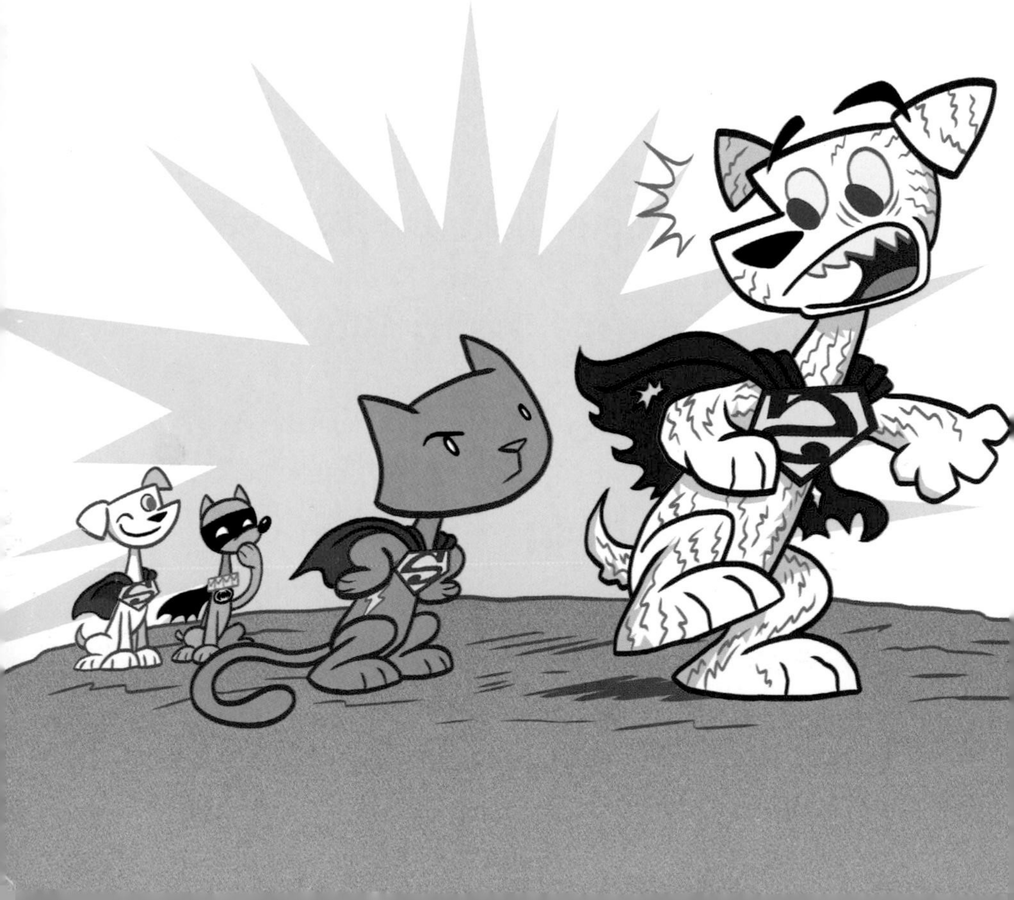

"He's afraid of cats!" Krypto said

aloud, trying not to laugh.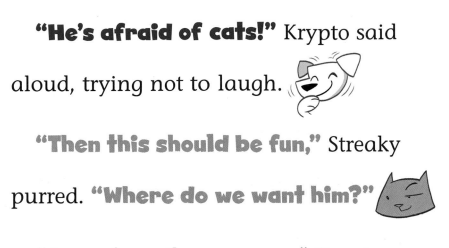

"Then this should be fun," Streaky

purred. **"Where do we want him?"**

"Away from the museum," Krypto

answered.

ZOOOMM!

Streaky flew right at Bizarro Krypto.

The frightened dog launched himself

at top speed. He fled toward the clouds.

The real Krypto and Streaky flew after

him. They had him on the run!

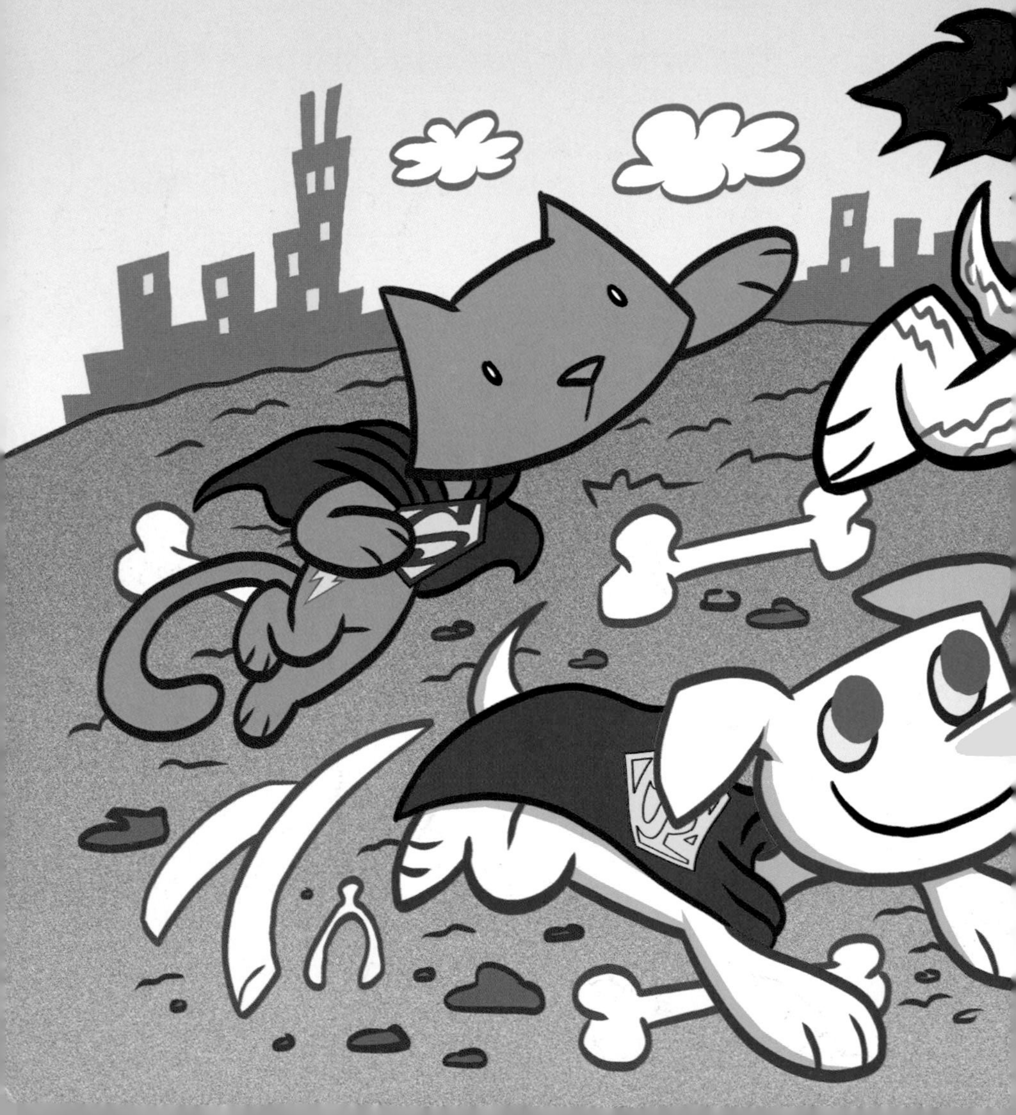

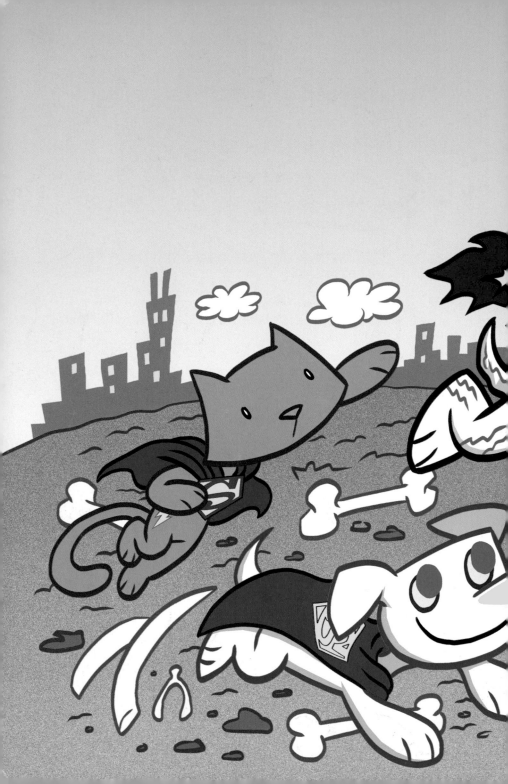

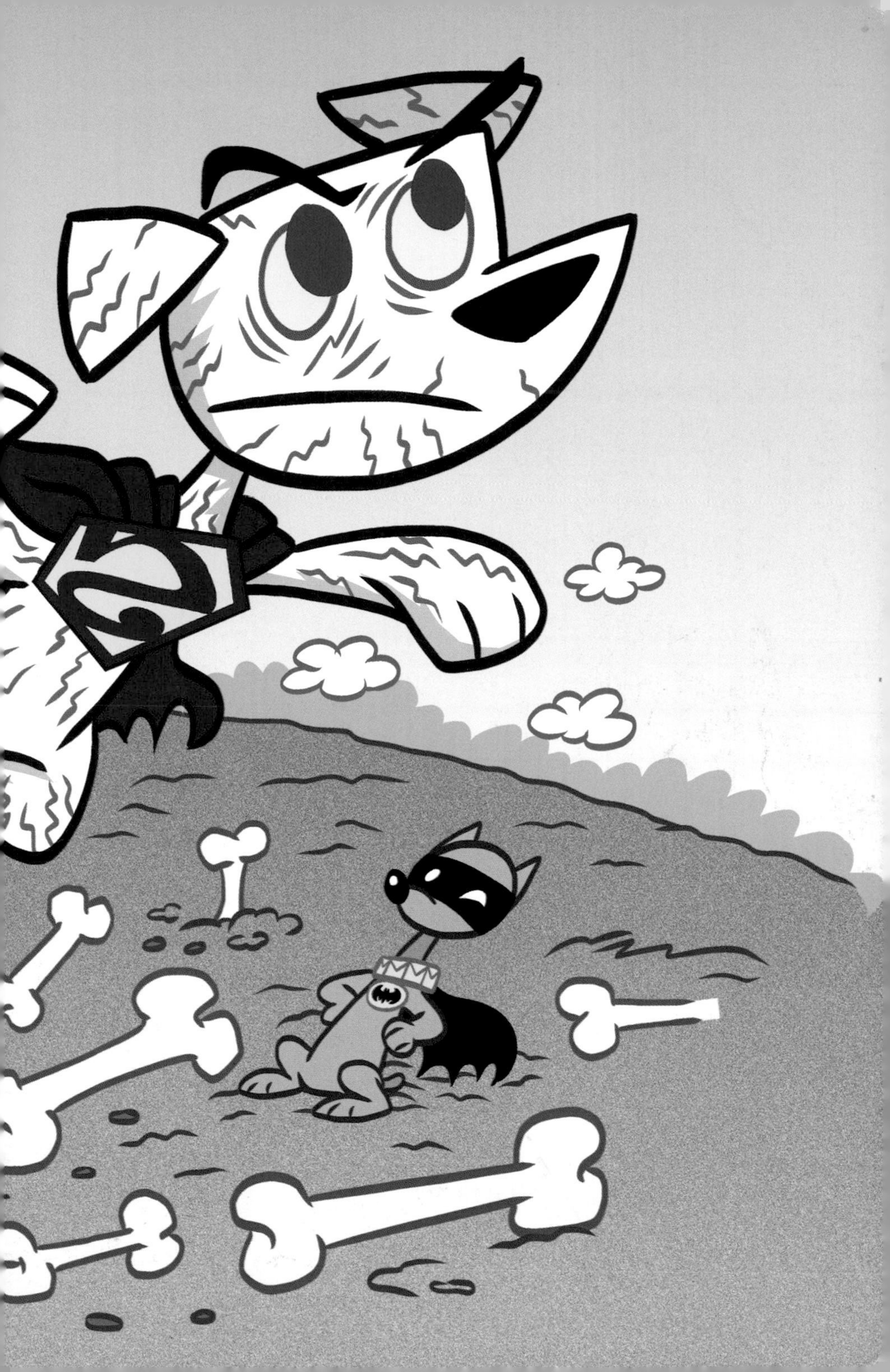

"This is purrfect," Streaky shouted to Krypto. He flexed his claws. **"But what should we do now?"**

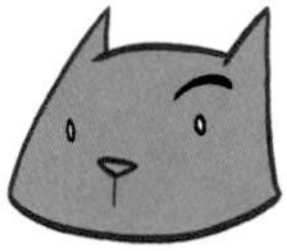

Krypto sniffed the air. Ace was nearby. **He pricked up his ears — Ace was calling to them!**

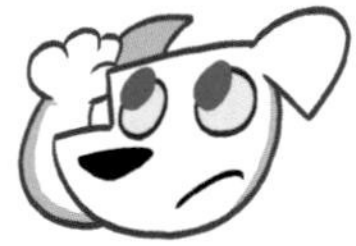

"Chase him this way," Krypto said.

Streaky picked up the pace and chased Bizarro Krypto in the new direction. In moments, they were in the parking lot where Bizarro Krypto had crash-landed.

DC™

SUPER-PETS!

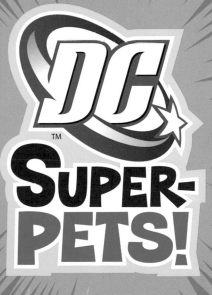

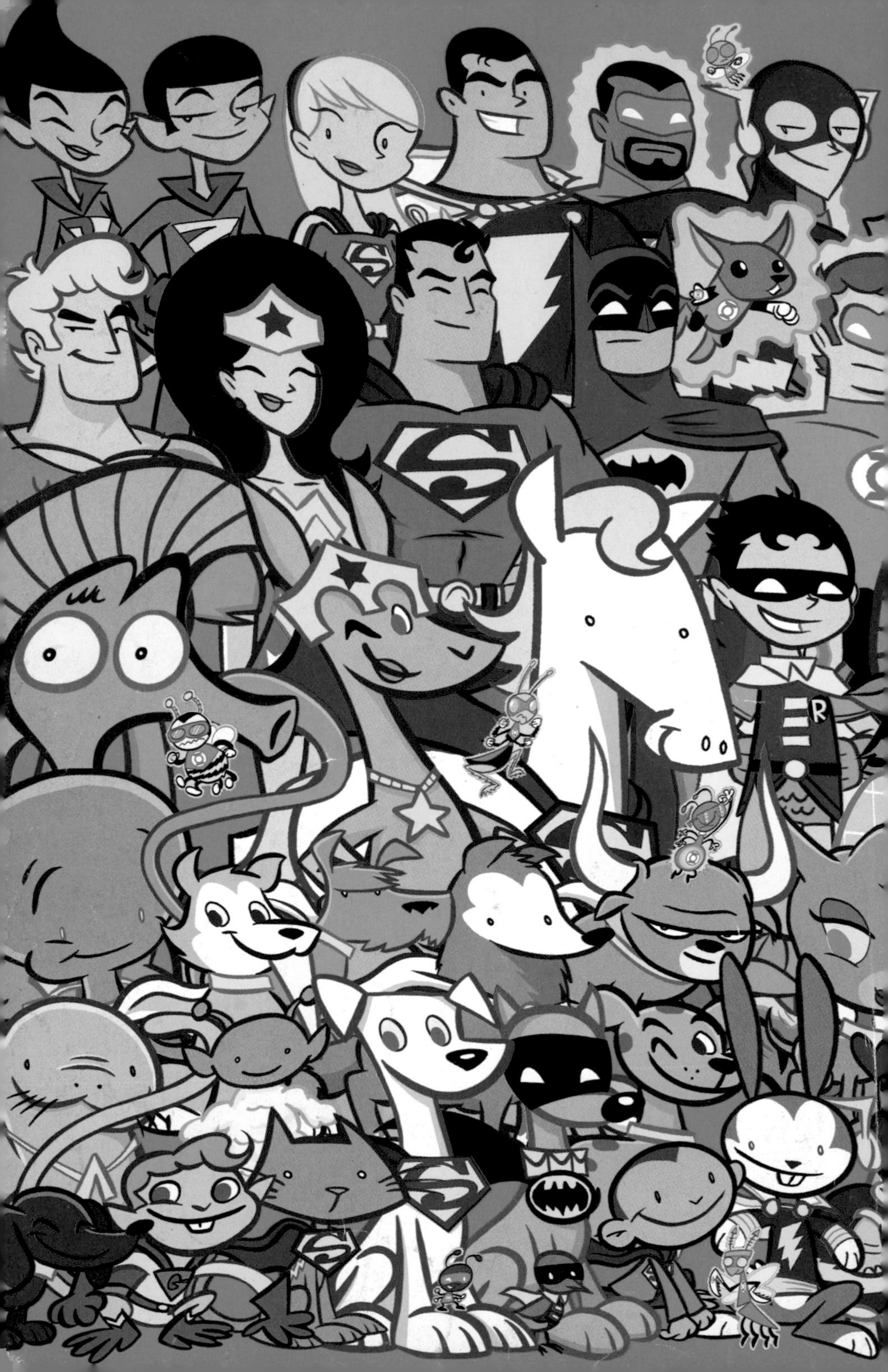

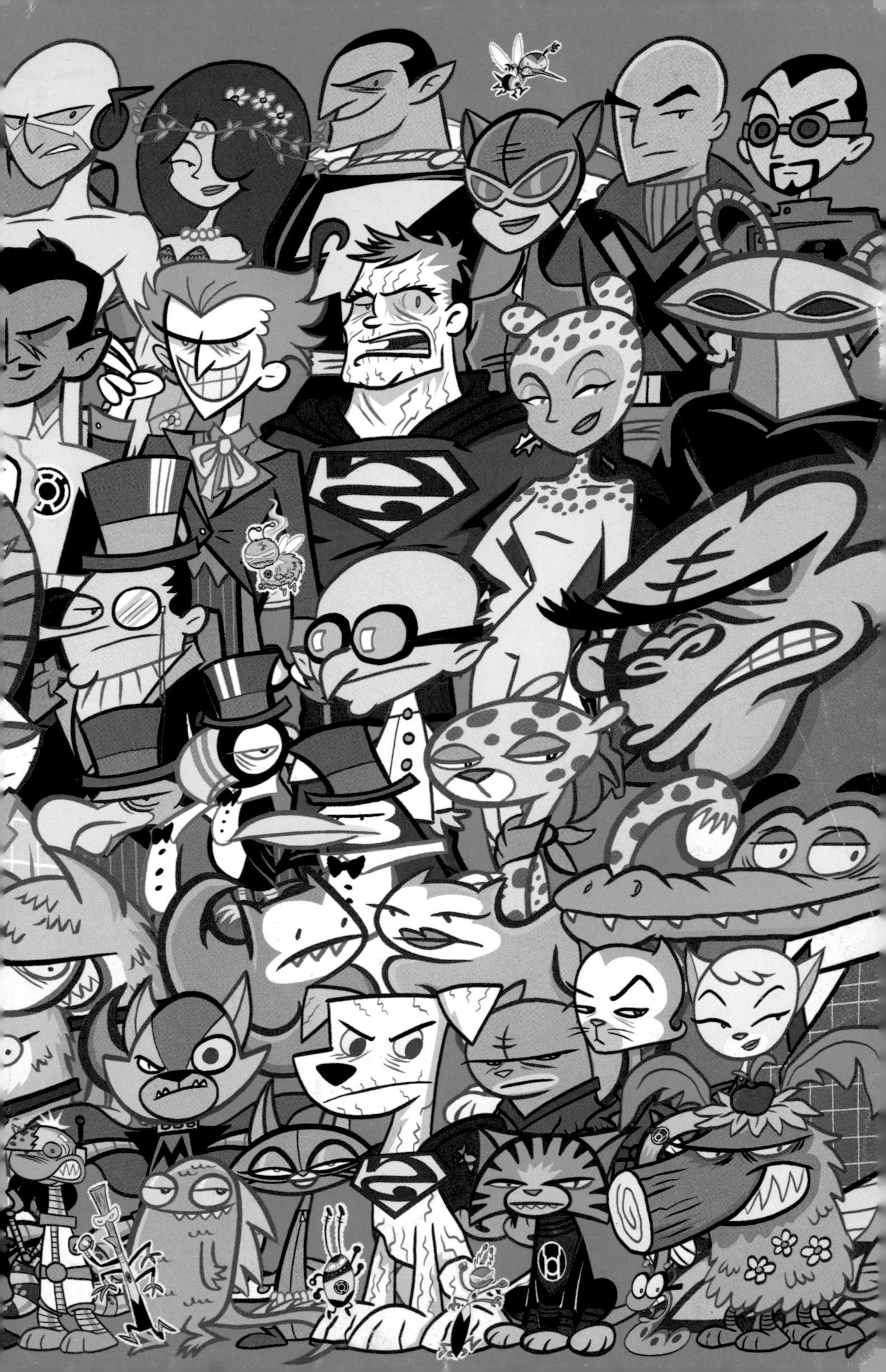

DC™ SUPER-PETS!

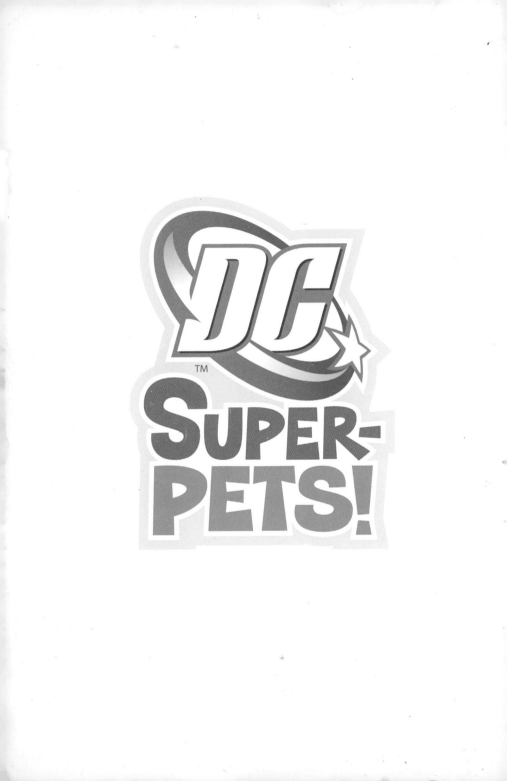